Parents and Caregivers,

Stone Arch Readers are designed to provide enjoyable reading experiences, as well as opportunities to develop vocabulary, literacy skills, and comprehension. Here are a few ways to support your beginning reader:

• Talk with your child about the ideas addressed in the story.

• Discuss each illustration, mentioning the characters, where they are, and what they are doing.

• Read with expression, pointing to each word. You may want to read the whole story through and then revisit parts of the story to ensure that the meanings of words or phrases are understood.

• Talk about why the character did what he or she did and what your child would do in that situation.

• Help your child connect with characters and events in the story.

Remember, reading with your child should be fun, not forced. Each moment spent reading with your child is a priceless investment in his or her literacy life.

Gail Saunders-Smith, Ph.D.

Stone Arch Readers

are published by Stone Arch Books
a Capstone Imprint
1710 Roe Crest Drive
North Mankato, Minnesota 56003
www.capstonepub.com

Library of Congress Cataloging-in-Publication Data
Yasuda, Anita.
Ghost sounds / by Anita Yasuda ; illustrated by Steve Harpster.
p. cm. -- (Stone Arch readers: Dino detectives)
Summary: When Dot the Diplodocus hears noises at night she thinks there is
a ghost in the house--and when her brother dismisses her fears the other
Dino Detectives decide to investigate.
ISBN 978-1-4342-4152-8 (library binding) -- ISBN 978-1-4342-4831-2 (pbk.)
1. Dinosaurs--Juvenile fiction. 2. Brothers and sisters--Juvenile fiction. [1. Dinosaurs--Fiction. 2. Brothers
and sisters--Fiction. 3. Mystery and detective stories.] I. Harpster, Steve, ill. II. Title.
PZ7.Y2124Gho 2013
813.6--dc23
2012026690

Reading Consultants:
Gail Saunders-Smith, Ph.D.
Melinda Melton Crow, M.Ed.
Laurie K. Holland, Media Specialist

Designer: Russell Griesmer

Printed in the United States of America in North Mankato, Minnesota.
042016
009742R

by **Anita Yasuda**
illustrated by **Steve Harpster**

STONE ARCH BOOKS
a capstone imprint

Meet the
Dino Detectives!

Dot the
Diplodocus

Sara the
Triceratops

Cory the
Corythosaurus

Ty the
T. rex

It is late at night. Everyone is sleeping but Dot.

Dot hears strange noises. She holds Teddy.

Dot looks in the closet. Nothing is there.

Dot checks under the bed.
Nothing is there.

"Is it Mom?" Dot asks Teddy.

But Dot's mom is sleeping.

"Is it Dad?" Dot asks Teddy.

But Dot's dad is sleeping.

Dot goes to her brother's room.

"What is it, Dot?" he asks.

"Did you hear that noise?" asks Dot.

"No," he says. "Go back to bed."

The next night, Dot's friends
come over. She tells them about
the strange noises.

"I think it's a ghost," says Dot.

"The Dino Detectives can crack this case," says Sara.

Sara puts flour on the floor.

"Do ghosts leave tracks?"
asks Dot.

"We'll see," says Sara.

Ty sets up a camera.

"Will we see a ghost in a picture?" asks Dot.

"We'll see," says Ty.

Cory sets out pizza.

"Do ghosts eat pizza?" asks Dot.

"We'll see," says Cory.

They go back to Dot's room and wait for the ghost. They wait and wait.

Then they hear a strange
noise.

"It's the ghost!" says Dot.

They creep out of Dot's room.

"Look!" says Dot. "There are tracks in the flour."

They tiptoe down the stairs.

"Look!" says Ty. "The camera fell down!"

They slowly open the kitchen door.

"Look!" says Sara. "Ghosts do
eat pizza!"

"And so does your brother,"
says Cory.

"I sure do! I have a snack every night," he says.

"Mystery solved," says Ty.

"No ghost, extra pizza, and a solved mystery," says Dot. "What a great night!"

"I agree," says her brother.

STORY WORDS

detectives   ghost   mystery

noises   camera   solved

Total Word Count: 267